CHANGING
FORTH   TUE

To Freya, without whom this book would never have happened.

With love, Mummy

First published in Great Britain in 2002 by Bloomsbury Publishing Plc
38 Soho Square, London, W1D 3HB

A CIP catalogue record of this book is available from the British Library
ISBN 0 7475 5021 2

Designed by Sarah Hodder

Printed in Singapore by Tien Wah Press

1 3 5 7 9 10 8 6 4 2

Mummy, Don't Go Out Tonight

Sally Gardner

BLOOMSBURY
CHILDREN'S
BOOKS

"Mummy, Mummy,
don't go out tonight."

"You will be all right.
Daisy will be here."

"Why can't I come with you?"

'Because it's night time
and night time is grown-up time."

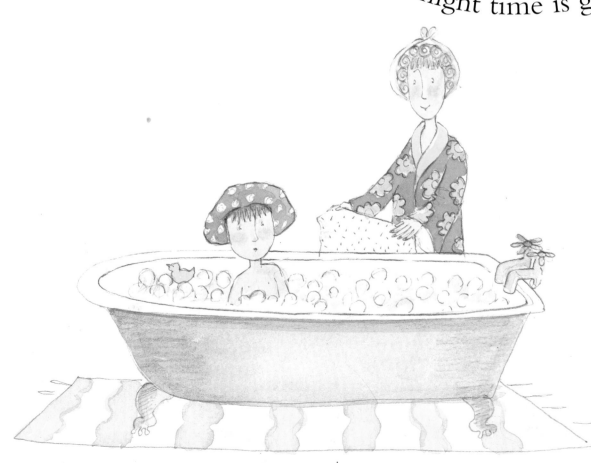

"But I need you all the time."

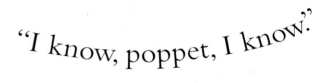

"I know, poppet, I know."

"Monster's going to miss you.
Cat's going to miss you."

"The house will feel so funny without you. I am going to miss you so so so."

"Give me a kiss now. I have to go."

"Mummy, don't go. There's a dragon under the stairs."

"No, poppet, only the hoover lives there."

"Mummy, you might be kidnapped by pirates."

"No, darling, there are no pirates where I'm going."

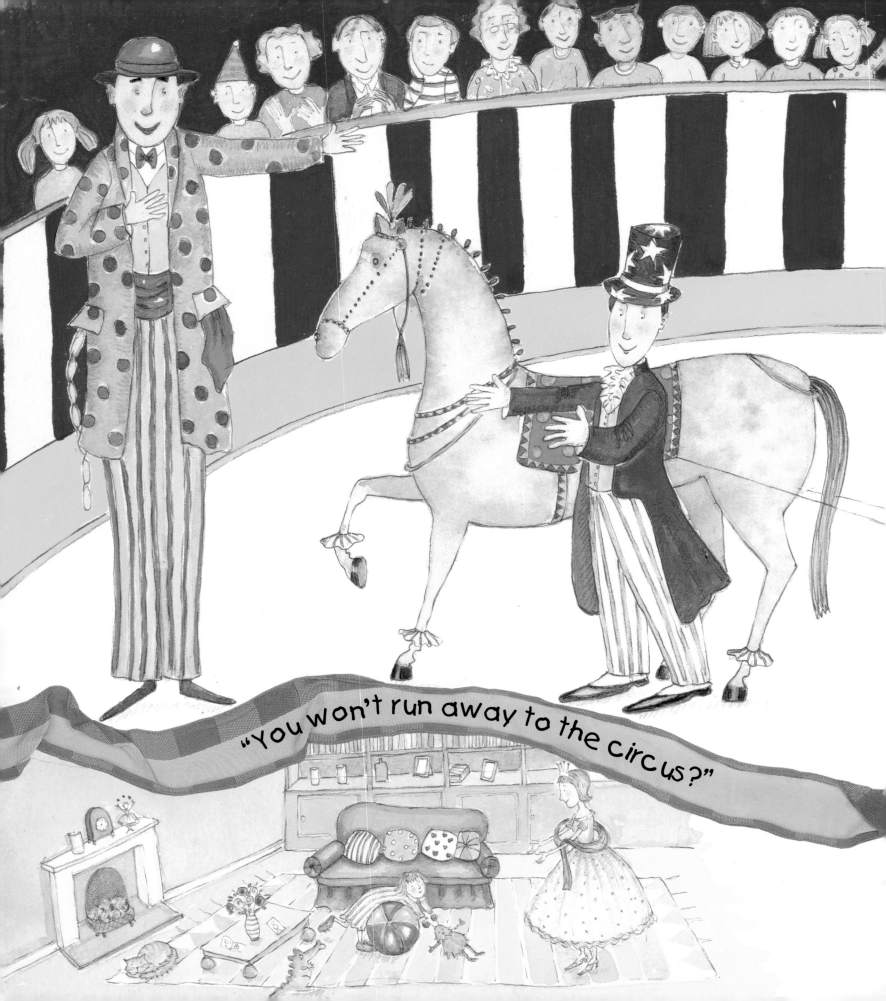

"You won't run away to the circus?"

"Poppet, don't be silly. No circus would have me!"

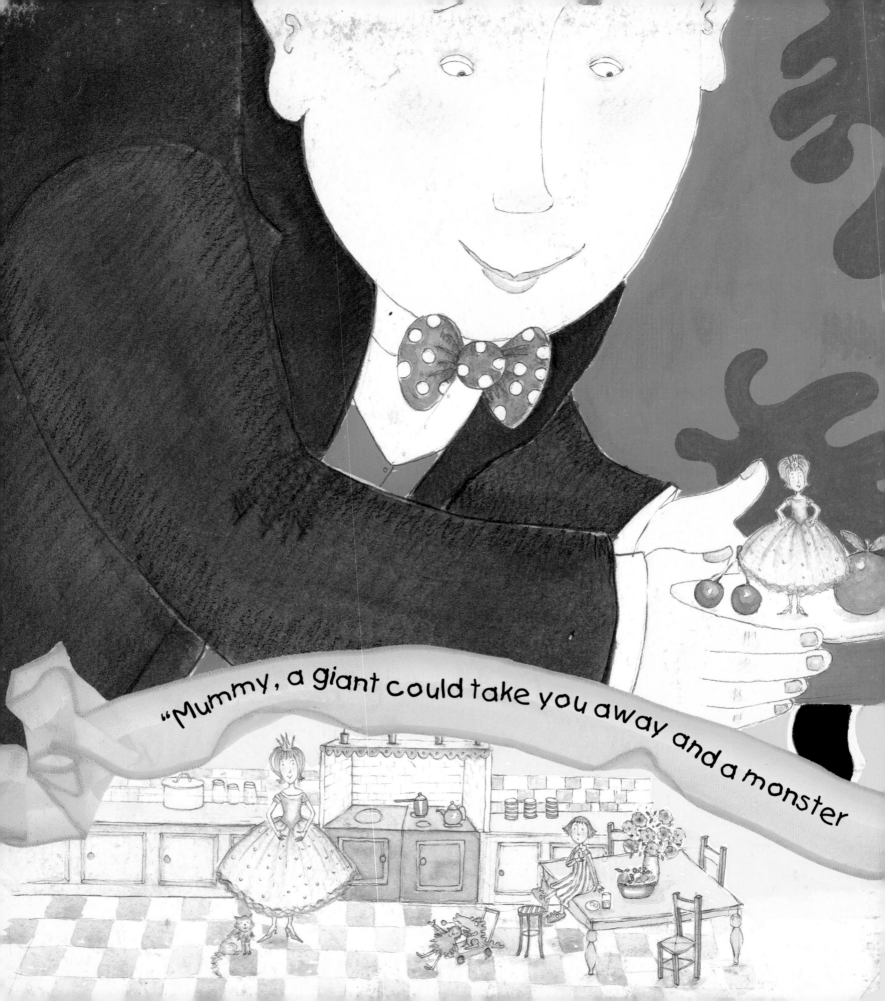

"Mummy, a giant could take you away and a monster

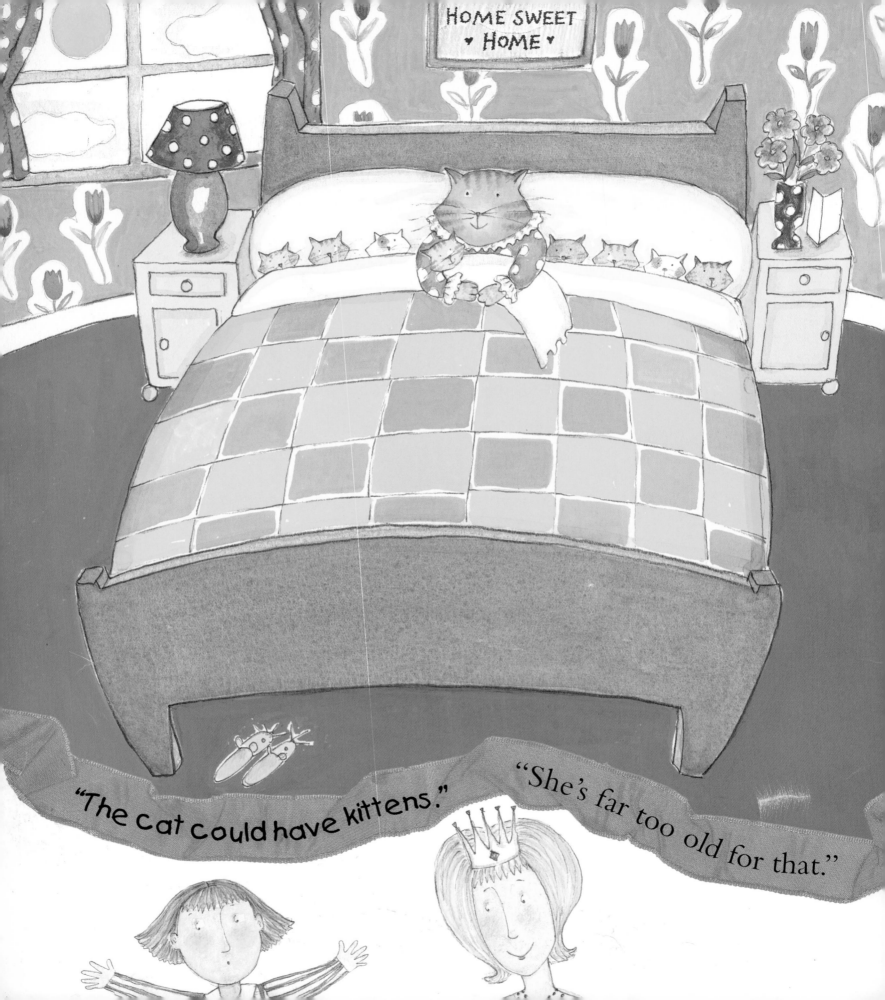

"The cat could have kittens." "She's far too old for that."

"Darling, everything is going to be all right.
Give me a kiss! Night-night."

"Daisy, may I have four fishfingers?

One for me and two for Monster and one for my dragon."

"Daisy, shall we go dancing? I will dress up.

I'll be a princess and you can be the prince."

"Daisy, will you read to me? This book and another one?

Is it long now, till Mummy is home?"

"Daisy, will you come again? Monster likes you being here,

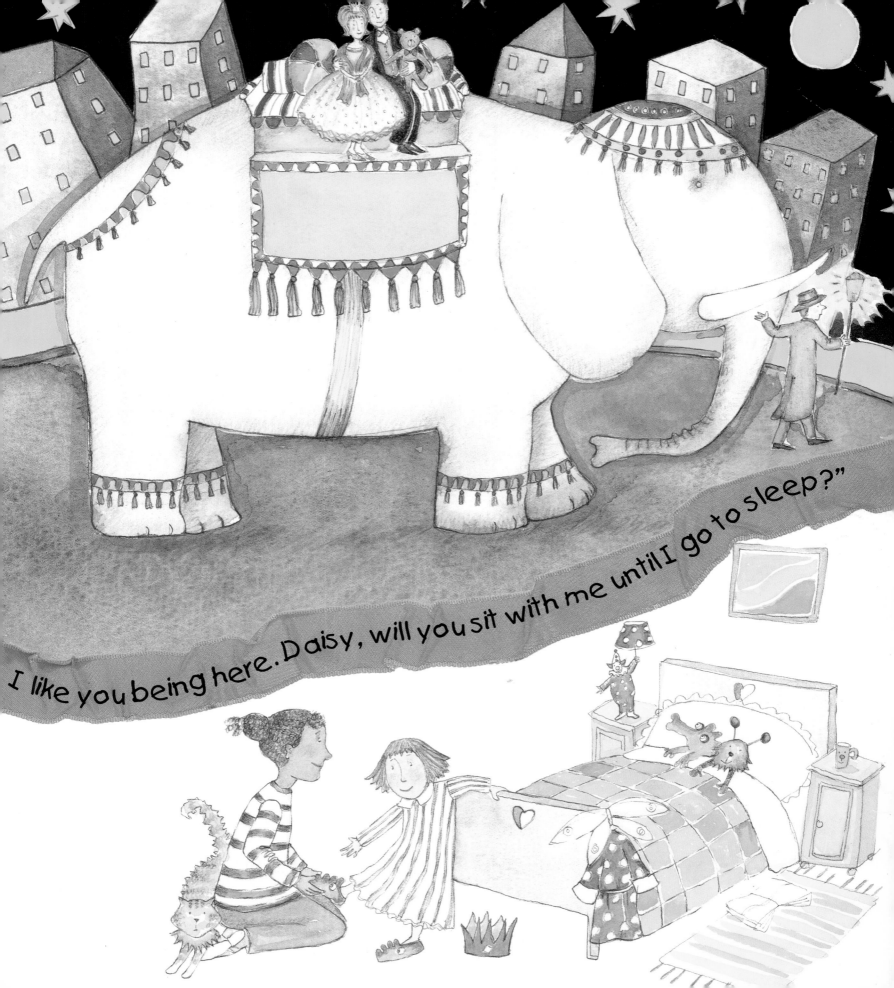

I like you being here. Daisy, will you sit with me until I go to sleep?"

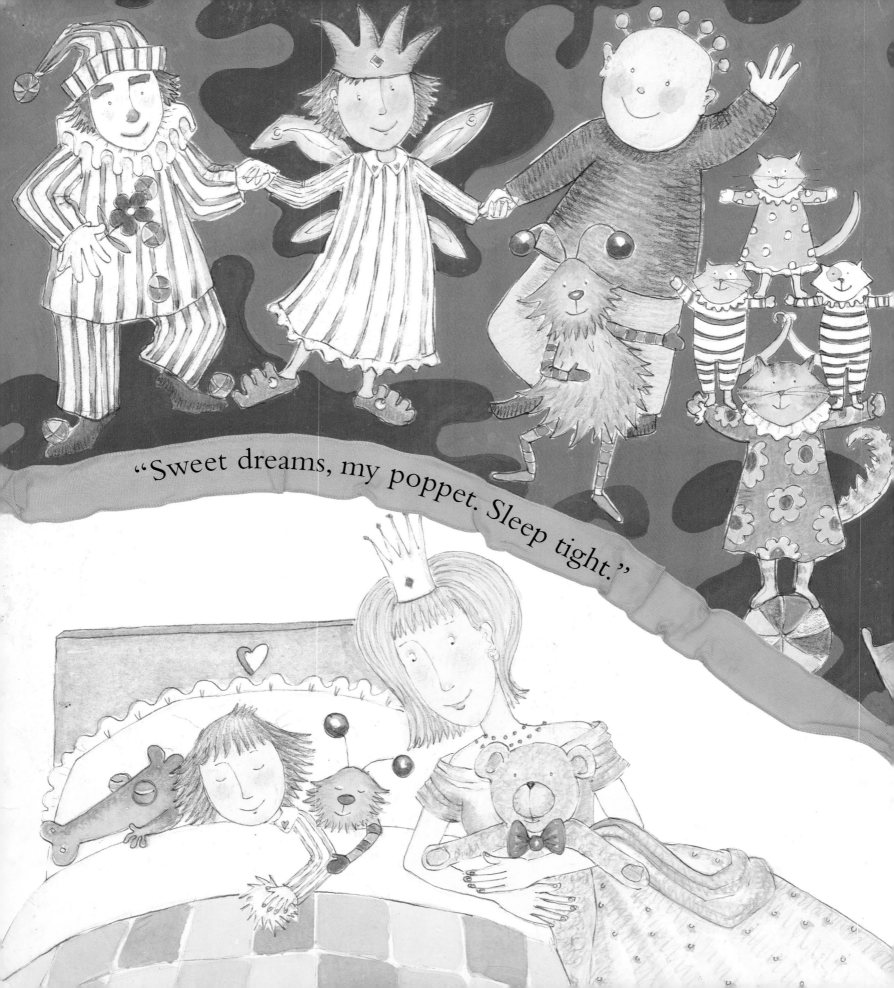

"Sweet dreams, my poppet. Sleep tight."